GW01086490

Caspar's dream

Bartholomew on the road

Caroline Moulinet

Illustrated by Sylvaine de Gantès

Caspar's dream

To Thérèse and Céline

To Martin

Caspar's dream

Bartholomew on the road

Caroline Moulinet

Illustrated by Sylvaine de Gantès

One night...

Caspar had spent a long day. A tiring one. On that Wednesday, he had gone to play basketball with his friend Martin after school. It had done him good after the morning without recess. The chatter in the classroom had made his teacher angry. Caspar was so annoyed by those few who made the whole class be punished. Why didn't they stop before things got bad? Really, it annoyed him to miss the games in the playground because of a handful of trouble makers. Now Caspar was in bed and looking for sleep. His thoughts went round and round in his head. He was replaying the events of this morning, changing one part or another to imagine all the possible conclusions. It was no use, it only prevented him from falling asleep, but he couldn't do otherwise.

At the end of the corridor, he could hear the muffled voices of Mum and Dad talking, he could hear the melody of the music coming from his sister's room a little louder. Madeleine was four years older than him so she was allowed to stay up later. Mum and Dad agreed to the music in the evening because they said Madeleine was becoming a teenager. Soon thirteen years old. The age of music to help falling asleep. Perhaps it would have helped Caspar? He had not reached that age and was looking for sleep in the quiet of his room. He looked for the lines of light around him. Daddy had often told him: "To fall asleep, Caspar, start by closing your eyes", but it was so hard to close his eyes and not listen to the sounds of the house when his thoughts kept turning in his head.

Caspar rolled over in bed once more, glancing at the alarm clock which was giving off a faint blue halo. His body was getting heavier on the mattress, the duvet warmer, his breath more regular. His eyelids were closed now, Caspar was entering dreamland. Then the adventure began...

The start

There, in a beautiful garden, he sees a young boy dressed as a knight. He is playing with a fawn, running after it, trying to catch it. The young fawn, full of energy, jumps from left to right laughing while the knight exclaims, "Matteus, wait for me, you're going too fast!" But Matteus seems to be having so much fun that he continues his crazy race and retorts, "You hurry up, Bartholomew! I tell you that the meadow over there is the best place I have found to play!" And the young boy runs faster and faster, holding his sword firmly so as not to lose it in the grass.

Matteus and Bartholomew live in an extraordinary garden. They play, they talk, they laugh, they also rest. They are not alone. They are accompanied by a little lamb whose name is Fileo. Fileo does not speak much, but he is a faithful friend, always there with them, and all the tenderness of heaven can be read in his eyes. This little group enjoys each day, together in the midst of the wonders that surround them. One of these wonders is their sweet friend Princess Anne-Marie. Anne-Marie often sits on the rock over there with her book on her lap. She says it is a wonderful book containing a thousand treasures of happiness. Bartholomew, on the other hand, doesn't like to spend time reading, he prefers to draw his sword, to walk through the garden, to imagine countless adventures of conquerors and victories. He has the spirit of the victorious, the strength of the bold, and the perseverance of the brave.

However, one day, after a beautiful morning of games, frantic races and shared laughter, a new animal creeps into the wonderful garden. It has a sly smile and treacherous eyes. Fortunately, Anne-Marie sees him sneak in. Her beautiful golden yellow dress flies in the wind as she runs towards Bartholomew and Matteus. She runs so fast that she is out of breath to share the news:

"My friends, beware, I have just seen the mischievous snake waving in the tall grass. I know it, I read it in my book: it is neither benevolent nor of good intention. I also know that a huge castle awaits us at the end of this path where we will be safe. My friends, do you want us to walk together? Let us make haste, the road is long, but happiness awaits us there!"

Gently, Fileo gazes at each member of this joyful troop. The knight Bartholomew grabs his sword and slips it into its scabbard. The fawn Matteus starts walking at his side. Princess Anne-Marie's smile shines brightly as she walks with her friends. The little lamb Fileo trots ahead. They are ready for adventure.

Chapter 1

The knight Bartholomew is determined to find the wonderful castle his friend the princess has been talking about. Bartholomew is a brave knight, a huge palace will be perfect for him! There's no way he's going to stay in their lovely garden, however beautiful it may be, if this ugly snake comes to spoil their games, interfere in their conversations, disrupt their laughter, and even disturb their rest. Moreover Bartholomew trusts his friend Anne-Marie who is so silent and spends so much time immersed in her book, he knows that she knows many secrets of happiness. Bartholomew is really happy to be on this journey with her and all their friends. The snake can always sneak in, but that won't stop their quest! "Beautiful castle, here we come!"

In his dreams of grandeur, conquest and victory, the knight Bartholomew does not see the big rock in the distance. It is huge and blocks the way.

In his thoughts, Bartholomew also fails to see the beauty of the landscape unfolding before his eyes. The birds nesting in the trees, their melodious songs, the light playing in the foliage. On the other hand, Princess Anne-Marie delights in the sounds of nature, the scents of the trees and the sparkling light. She follows the path with her fellow walkers and guesses in the distance the big rock that blocks the passage.

"Bartholomew, my friend, look ahead!" But Bartholomew is far too busy: he is trying to hang up the buttons on his beautiful knight's uniform. The second golden button is about to come off, so something must be done: what is a disheveled knight?

The team continues to walk, Bartholomew is still concentrating on the buttons of his uniform. With one hand, he holds his sword, with the other he pokes at the button to see how much longer it will hold. He is no longer listening to his friends' conversation, he can only hear them talking when suddenly, BAM! Ouch! He is hit! Knocked down!... Sitting on the ground, his butt in the dust. He hit the huge rock that was blocking the road. Concentrated as he was on his beautiful knight's uniform, he forgot the way. He is in pain, a large bump is growing rapidly on his forehead like a daffodil in spring. His friends look at him and ask, "Did you hurt yourself?"

"Of course I did! What a question! Look at this bump and my beautiful uniform covered in dust!" shouts the angry knight.

Here is the valiant knight Bartholomew sulking... He crosses his arms, frowning. He doesn't even want to get up: it's not his fault that he fell! It was that big, stupid rock that caused it all!

No, Bartholomew really doesn't want to get up anymore. He wants to stay there, sulking, brooding, replaying in his head the grotesque scene of this beautiful and joyful troop advancing straight towards the rock.

"Fileo, what have you done? Why didn't you tell me?" accuses Bartholomew.

Fileo looks tenderly at the knight and replies, "My friend, we are walking together, I am at your side. The big rock was blocking the way, we slowed down, you didn't stop, you ran into it just because you were looking at the buttons on your belly".

Matteus comes closer. Princess Anne-Marie reaches out to Bartholomew to help him stand up and adjust his uniform. Even dusty, it is wonderful in her eyes. She smiles at her friend.

"Pff...," says the knight, "I've been silly." Bartholomew gives a half-smile.

"Pff and pff... this beautiful bump will remind me to look around and listen to your wise advice. It's true that I forgot about you for a while to take care of my buttons. Let's go around that rock! Come on, let's get going!"

Happy is the one who has the simplicity to smile at himself,

He has not finished laughing!

This treasure of life is called humility.

Chapter 2

Bartholomew, the fawn Matteus and Princess Anne-Marie continue on their way, with the little lamb Fileo always at the front of this joyful group. The knight rubs his hump while accepting the teasing of his friends, the princess shares the wonders she enjoys contemplating around her. Matteus bounces from left to right with laughter. And Fileo is there, silent and smiling, happy about this adventure together.

Suddenly, a strong flash of light dazzles the knight. There, in the grass at the foot of the cherry tree, something shines and catches his eye. "Wait! Let's go and see!" he exclaims.

At the foot of the tree Bartholomew found a golden coin. How beautiful it is! It shines so brightly in the sun that it stings his eyes! "Wait! Perhaps there are others!"

Indeed, going around the tree, Bartholomew finds another coin, then another. Three beautiful coins that he slips into the pocket of his uniform. He wants to look again and again, to search the grass a little more, to find other treasures, but the princess intervenes, "Bartholomew, my friend, let's not stay here any longer. We have everything we need for our journey, let's continue our quest, the castle is still waiting for us far down the road."

"But that's just it, Anne-Marie," retorted the knight, "the road is long, and we need to be sure that we have everything we need to continue the journey! Let's look again! Let's not go any further until we are sure we have found all the gold coins!"

So the companions, eager to help their friend, search with their hands or feet, hooves or noses, to find all the gold coins scattered at the foot of the tree. They are all still bent over looking when a boy comes along the path from another direction. He looks very tired, his clothes are wrinkled and his sandals reveal his red and tired feet. The friends stop their search and the princess asks, "Hello traveller, what is your name? And what are you doing here so late?"

"My name is Balthazar, I am walking this path in search of a star. But look at my tiredness and my damaged feet, would you have some water and maybe some new shoes?"

Matteus approaches and offers the pouch strapped to his side. "The water is there, drink and rest."

The princess looks at her knight friend, his uniform, his sword... and his boots. Discreetly, she slips into his ear, "Bartholomew, brave knight, don't you think you should help him? Why don't you exchange your boots for Balthazar's sandals? His poor feet will be able to heal, and you, with all the gold you've just found, can always buy other boots further down the road. What do you think, my friend?"

Bartholomew doesn't want to give his boots away at all, they go so well with his uniform. He doesn't know this man, and what if he needs his gold coins to face the dangers of the road rather than to replace old sandals?

The princess whispers to him again, "Bartholomew, you'll look even better in my eyes with your toes in the air!"

Ah this princess has a knack for finding funny formulas! So Bartholomew, brave knight, accepts the deal. And to remember this funny experience, he invents another funny formula:

Sobriety and generosity are good qualities

On the road to progress,

My sandals will turn into my best allies

On the way together here comes success

The knight takes off his boots and settles comfortably on the grass a little way off the path. He invites his companions, "Come on, let's rest now. It's dusk, let's share a meal. Balthazar will tell us about the star he is looking for and we will regain our strength before continuing our journey tomorrow."

Anne-Marie prepares the meal, Matteus lies down in a circle, snuggled up against his friend's petticoats, and Balthazar begins to tell all about his quest. The knight Bartholomew, while listening attentively, looks at the sandals he has just exchanged. These sandals have already come a long way... In the peace that suddenly penetrates his heart, he senses that this exchange will bring him even greater happiness.

Happy is the one who knows how to find the impetus to share,

He will move forward on the path with a light heart.

This treasure of life is called generosity.

Chapter 3

The next morning, the friends wake up to the sound of birdsong. Balthazar prepares to continue his journey, once again thanking Bartholomew for his comfortable boots. The merry band gathers their belongings and continues on their way to the wonderful castle that Anne-Marie has promised.

Fileo always leads the way when he starts to slow down. Bartholomew gets closer and discovers a passageway in front of him that weaves its way between two hills. Matteus and Anne-Marie having joined them, they look together at the landscape in front of them. The light makes the last dewdrops shine and they hear the sound of a waterfall in the distance. The knight takes the time to linger over the details of the road. Several stones litter the ground. For him, who is now wearing sandals, it will be a question of not slipping: the wet stones can be treacherous. Fileo seems to question Bartholomew with his eyes. The knight says to him, "The passage is not as easy as it seems. Let us go forward slowly." So the little lamb resumes his walk.

Bartholomew is right, the stones are slippery. Fileo advances painfully, his hooves often slip, but he keeps his soft and tender gaze. The fawn Matteus imitates him and puts his hooves in the same places as his friend. The knight progresses with difficulty, he feels his ankles twist several times, the pain is slight but unpleasant. His toes are icy. This gully is a very wet passage. He turns around and sees Anne-Marie behind, falling behind the group. He stops and waits for her. He waits for her and his mind starts to wander. What if Anne-Marie fell? How would he carry her on his back? They would both fall on the slippery stones, that's for sure. And she was the one who had advised him to change his boots! That was really not smart! She was going to get hurt and so was he, and it was her fault!

The knight let his imagination run wild and his anger rose faster than a mountain stream at the melting of the winter snows. Like a torrent, his anger thunders and roars inside him. Bartholomew cries out, "Move, damn it! What are you doing back there? Don't ask me to come and get you, you're the one who advised me to give my boots away! And couldn't your brilliant book show us a better way?"

Anne-Marie is too far back to hear the knight's words but she can sense his anger. Bartholomew is making big gestures, he seems quite agitated. She continues to move forward, step by step, calmly to keep her balance and not to drop her wonderful book on the wet ground. When she finally gets close enough to the knight to hear his words, she is startled. What is happening to her friend? Just a few minutes ago they were all together deciding how to move forward on this winding path between the hills, all focused and peaceful. Now Bartholomew's cheeks are flushed with anger, he is ranting and raving. He shouts, "You'd better be right about your castle story, because we're in big trouble! We're all going to slip and break our bones! Your fault!" The princess takes a breath, the morning air tastes fresh. She looks ahead at Fileo and Matteus who are moving forward, haphazardly. They don't look agitated despite their small steps. Anne-Marie replies, "Bartholomew, my friend, I didn't fall, nor did our friends. You yourself seem to be standing well, on your own two feet. Why are you getting so upset?" The knight replies, "That's just it! They don't wait for me, and with every step I can hurt myself by slipping in my sandals. Besides, I'm waiting for you to help you and you don't even see that I'm there for you! Why does no one ever see my efforts? And first of all, I want to stop everything and go back to our garden where there was no risk of falling!"

Anne-Marie's heart is moved by the knight's distress. He is overcome with anger, standing there motionless, each of his feet balanced on a wet pebble. How wise the princess is: she sees deeper into her friend's heart, beyond his anger. Gently, she replies, "Bartholomew, they managed to get through with their hooves, we'll manage with our two feet.

Come on, let's move on. I'm not going fast, but I'm going steadily, I don't want to let go of my book. I won't let go of you either. And I thank you for waiting for me, I'm happy to walk with you. Look over there, Fileo and Matteus are waiting for us too. The difficult part is almost over."

Anne-Marie's voice has calmed Bartholomew's heart a little. They move on together. The day is progressing and the stones are gradually drying. Their progress becomes easier. They walk towards Fileo and Matteus. When they have only a hundred metres to go, the knight gently takes his friend's hand and says softly, "Sorry, Anne-Marie. I'm sorry I got upset. I was afraid, afraid of being alone and not being able to do it. I'm glad we got through." The princess smiles at her friend. They move forward serenely as Matteus's voice echoes, "Friends, come and see this! It's so beautiful!"

Small stream or raging torrent,
anger can sometimes carry everything away.

Happy is the one who finds the gentleness
and kindness to calm down.

This treasure of life is called serenity.

Chapter 4

The knight and the princess join Matteus who seems to be very excited. He exclaims again, "It's so beautiful! Look!" He is right. Fileo is there, and before him unfolds a wonderful meadow. The humidity of the narrow path changes into a clear stream. A little further on, a lake shines in the midday sun. The emerald green grass has a minty scent. To the left of the lake grow many splendid fruit trees. Bartholomew is speechless as he contemplates this prodigious meadow. Tears of happiness fill his eyes. This meadow reminds him of his beloved garden and being here warms his heart. He takes off his sandals and walks barefoot in the soft grass. He tries to guess in the branches where the nests of the birds are that sing with such a beautiful voice. He breathes in the fragrance of this green setting before sitting down by the water, resting his feet in the lake. Anne-Marie looks at him and smiles. She sits down a little way off, under a fragrant pine tree that offers her its shade. She immerses herself with delight in reading her wonderful book. The fawn Matteus leaps from left to right and has fun chasing butterflies. And the little lamb Fileo, standing on the hill, rejoices for his friends.

Bartholomew looks at his feet in the clear water. This water seems warm to him after walking on the wet path. Everything is beautiful in this meadow. The water is shining, the grass is waving in the wind, birds are singing, butterflies are fluttering. Even the trees seem to be bearing fruit without worrying about the influence of the seasons. The knight can see kiwis, apples, pears, strawberries, raspberries. Their next meal already looks excellent!

He looks at every corner of this enchanted place, and he hears Anne-Marie's sweet voice humming a familiar tune. Anne-Marie sings when she feels good. Bartholomew smiles when he sees her there, immersed in her wonderful book. All this reminds him of his beautiful garden. Yet his heart is not nostalgic; on the contrary, he feels comforted, cuddled. A strange feeling, as if someone was looking after his path. At that moment, the knight's eyes meet those of the lamb Fileo, standing on the hillside. His eyes, so soft, so tender and so deep, do not need words to express their affection. These few seconds have a taste of eternity. Then the fawn Matteus arrives, gambolling from left to right and says to his friend, "Bartholomew, come and play! I'll show you my great idea!" The knight stands up, smiling to himself: Matteus excels at inventing games, and he, as a good knight friend, is happy to have fun. He has the spirit of the victorious, the strength of the bold, and the perseverance of the brave, and in their games, in this prodigious meadow, everything is possible.

Chapter 5

The companions spend a wonderful day and night in this prodigious meadow. The next morning, it is time to set off again. Knight Bartholomew feels vulnerable. He does not know why, he is not at peace. What is going on?

The merry group moves on, Princess Anne-Marie tells what she has read in her book about the great castle that awaits them. Fileo trots slightly ahead. Matteus is at his side. The weather is grey today, the breeze is cold. The path is easy, flat, covered with soft grass. Bartholomew walks listening. He looks ahead at Fileo and Matteus. His eyes rest on Matteus's hooves, and in his heart he envies his friend. He doesn't really know why, but he would like to be like him. Bartholomew moves on, listening to Anne-Marie. A gust of wind blows in his face. The path is so easy and so flat today, why does he, a valiant knight, feel so unsafe? His gaze still lingers on the ground and he sees the princess's feet. She walks as if the earth carried her, as if her weight were lighter than a feather. Why does he feel so heavy today?

Anne-Marie is silent, and continues walking beside Bartholomew. After a few minutes, she addresses her friend, "You are very quiet, Bartholomew, today." For all answer, the knight growls, "Hum hum…" The silence of his heart is as grey as the sky. Bartholomew continues to walk, not knowing if the cloud will pass. A new gust of wind, a few more steps, and suddenly: Ouch! A sharp stone gets into his sandal! Bartholomew gritted his teeth. This stone has taken him by surprise on this soft grass path! Like an electric sting entering his body through his feet. His "Ouch!" resounds louder in his heart.

The companions stop for a moment, Matteus offers the princess some water. Bartholomew's eyes are still fixed on the ground. His gaze goes up slowly, he sees Matteus's hooves, his gaze goes up again, he meets Fileo's. His eyes are so soft, full of tenderness and kindness. His eyes that never have an ounce of judgment. Bartholomew lowers his eyes to the ground again and says to himself, "Let's be honest, I'm jealous of my friend. And I'm even jealous of Anne-Marie today." He doesn't know what to do with the darkness in his heart, he doesn't know how to push back this electric sting that has reached his whole being. Once again Bartholomew straightens his gaze and meets Fileo's. The little lamb has such a look in his eyes that it is hard to imagine how he would have felt. The little lamb's eyes are so deep that he seems to be able to speak directly to the knight's heart and say to him softly, "Don't worry. Matteus was born with clogs, Anne-Marie has precious talents, and you can rejoice for them." Bartholomew hears Fileo speaking to his heart but he doesn't know how to do it. How can he rejoice when he wants to be in his friend's shoes? The valiant knight, so calm and silent, his lips sealed by his jealousy, hears in the privacy of his heart Fileo continue, "Don't worry. I will tell you the words. I will teach you to rejoice."

Anne-Marie has been drinking and is ready to walk. Matteus is waiting for Fileo to continue the adventure. Bartholomew silently keeps the words that his friend the lamb has written in his heart. His gaze rises for a moment to the sky. There, ahead, the light descends between the clouds like a path of light that reaches the ground. The companions set off again.

The courageous knight advances in silence. In his heart he looks at his desire. Matteus looks like Fileo with his clogs. He would like to be like him. But has anyone ever seen a knight with clogs on? He would no longer be able to run, brandish his sword and dream of adventures of conquerors and victories. Anne-Marie then? Bartholomew would like to have her light step. Can he manage to rejoice without desiring all these qualities for himself? He repeats in his heart. "Rejoice..."

Fileo stops and announces, "My friends, it is time to take a break, we will be fine here." Bartholomew is surprised to answer without thinking, "Wonderful! Thank you Matteus, I've been watching you walk and it's helped me to move forward." How about that! But it's true: watching Matteus's hooves in front of him allowed him to move forward calmly on this grassy path, without hesitation, without getting lost! And Anne-Marie and her light step? Yes, of course! It is thanks to her that he could see how flat and easy the path was today. He doesn't need the talents of his friends, these talents have served their whole merry team! This makes Bartholomew happy! Yes, he is delighted! His eyes meet Fileo's. The clouds open and Fileo is bathed in light, a light that envelops the whole joyful group. The brave knight is full of gratitude for the words his friend gave him, at the right time, just for him: yes, Bartholomew is rejoicing today.

Blessed is the one who chooses to bless others and rejoice in their qualities,

He will discover the treasure of his own beauty.

Chapter 6

After a much appreciated break, the friends set off again. Princess Anne-Marie reassured them that they had passed the halfway point! This is very encouraging! They will stop for lunch and rest in the afternoon. Another hour's walk, Knight Bartholomew is looking forward to the relaxing time ahead and is looking forward to playing with the fawn Matteus.

The friends have been walking for forty minutes now and the knight's stomach is starting to rumble. He can't wait for lunch! They arrive at a sand-covered passage. Bartholomew likes sand. He stops and takes off his sandals. It is so soft, the sand has warmed up in the sun, it slips between his toes. The sand offers a unique, pleasant and delicious sensation. Exquisite. Bartholomew walks and enjoys every step in the warm sand. Fileo, Matteus and Anne-Marie move forward, while the knight slows down. This sand is so pleasurable, it is perhaps the best part of the path! The knight does not tire: again and again he paces up and down. Each little grain of sand takes care of his feet, warms them, massages them. All the knight's senses are awake. He would like to stay there, to walk again and again, to walk only on the warm sand that envelops his feet.

The lamb, the fawn and the princess are waiting for Bartholomew. For today, they have finished the journey, it is time for lunch now. Bartholomew's belly can be heard again, but he cannot leave the delicious sand. He paces, he circles, he walks again, savouring the sensations that the sand offers him.

Finally, the knight decides to join his friends. The meal is ready, Bartholomew sits down and starts to eat. Anne-Marie corrects him, "My friend, don't hurry now. We have prepared lunch and we have been waiting for you." The brave knight puts down the slice he had grabbed, "I have savoured the sensations of the sand so much that I am starving! But you're right, Anne-Marie, that's no reason to eat first when you've prepared everything!" The princess smiles at her friend. Bartholomew is so moving, full of good will and as greedy for the warmth on his feet as for the delicious food that has been prepared! Anne-Marie laughs, "A measure of vigilance, a few grams of perseverance, let it rest for a few moments so that everyone is present: voilà, it's ready, enjoy!"

Happy is the one who knows how to control his desires,

He will taste the fraternity of friendship.

Chapter 7

The companions had a nice afternoon and a peaceful night. Anne-Marie wakes up first. She looks at her sleeping friends, lying on the grass. Fileo always exudes such tenderness. Even asleep, he seems to radiate softness, like a warm little baby sleeping in his cot. Matteus lies on his side not far from his friend. His breathing is peaceful. Bartholomew has settled at the foot of a tree whose foliage forms a canopy over his head. It is as if nature is making a real king's bed for his friend.

Anne-Marie sits up a little and continues to contemplate the nature that surrounds her. The sky is pink, the first birds are beginning to hum their morning song. The princess looks at her wonderful book, her treasure full of promises of happiness. A breath of wind opens the book. Anne-Marie leans over to look. Her book is so alive! It seems to her that it always has the answer to her questions, that it can guide her, reassure her, comfort her. She never finishes discovering it. Really, this book contains the secret of happiness.

A new breath of wind and a few pages turn. As usual, the princess, full of wisdom, lets the book show her the message it holds for her today. The silence of the morning is so auspicious. Even more than the sky lighting up, it is Anne-Marie's heart that finds the light by letting her book speak to her.

Anne-Marie is at peace. She smiles. She hears the breathing of her friends. She looks at the open page of her book and reads the passage given to her for that day. The princess does not know what the day will be like, yet it seems to her that her book gives her exactly what she needs each day. She is so happy, she feels such great joy inside, that her golden dress begins to glow. The glow awakens her friends from their torpor and they blink. Anne-Marie is sitting there, her book closed in her lap. She watches Fileo, Matteus and Bartholomew yawn, stretch, wake up. Her dress is back to its usual colour. The birds are singing a little louder now, as if to invite the happy company to start their day. They seem to be humming "Wake up, wake up! Wake up!" The sun is up now, the friends will continue walking.

Chapter 8

The companions prepare for the road, but Knight Bartholomew has trouble getting up. He feels good against his tree, he still wants to rest. In the grass, he hears a whistling sound that says to him, "You don't have to go on this road, stay here, rest. You have already walked so much, there is no need to go any further." Bartholomew is surprised; he does not yet see the beautiful castle that Anne-Marie has spoken of; he knows that he must still walk with his friends to find it. This castle is at the end of the road, that's for sure.

The whistling resumes, "No, relax, rest. Why do you want a big castle when this tree makes you like a king's bed? Stay here, with me. The castle doesn't matter. I'll do everything to make you feel as comfortable here as in the castle your friend mentioned. I have a thousand flavours and sensations to offer you. You really don't need to tire yourself out walking."

The brave and persevering Bartholomew hesitates. What is that strange voice? He is well here, it is true, but this is not the end of the road. Does he really need to discover the castle of which the princess speaks? The whistling in the grass seems to promise other wonders. Yet the knight does not feel calm. Nature is beautiful, the sun's rays are slowly beginning to warm his feet. As he looks at them, he thinks of the warm sand between his toes yesterday, he also remembers the clear water that had refreshed him in the prodigious garden the other day. Bartholomew hesitates. He looks at his sandals lying not far from him. He thinks of Balthazar with his tired feet. He shared his beautiful story and nothing was going to stop him on his way to find his star. The knight does not regret his boots at all, on the contrary, his light sandals invite him to look for his own star on this path.

The whistle interrupts the knight's thoughts and resumes louder, "There is no star or castle, stay there, I will take care of you!" These words are not a kind invitation, they are like an aggression. Bartholomew's heart sinks as his friend Anne-Marie exclaims, "Watch out Bartholomew! The snake, there!" Bartholomew is startled and he hears a crunching noise in the grass. He understands: he has just heard the snake. Hm... That explains why he didn't feel calm. He shivers, but realises that he is safe, accompanied by his friends. Anne-Marie approaches the knight and asks, "How are you my friend?" Bartholomew replies, "Better now, I have been off guard with that whistle... I'll be more vigilant!"

Fileo, standing, looks at Bartholomew under his tree.
He has not taken his eyes off him for a moment.

Happy is he who learns to recognise the voice of his friends,

He will not be deceived, he will remain faithful to the truth.

This treasure of life is called prudence.

Chapter 9

It has been a long road. It is the end now. The end is near, but the long road turns into a dark tunnel. Bartholomew is afraid. He knows that he now knows all the necessary treasures, that he is close to the desired goal, but he is afraid. What if he is about to face the hardest test of all? The one that will get the better of him, the one that will leave him on the ground, on the outskirts of the castle? What if the snake that made them leave their magnificent garden should come and entangle his feet? In the distance, he can make out the light, he hears the voices of his friends, but he can't quite define where to go. He looks for the sound of Fileo's hooves.

Now it is dark, darker than the moonless nights. So the valiant knight closes his eyes. He searches inside himself. He sees the path again, the stones, the treasures collected. He remembers all that road with his companions. The night that Bartholomew goes through does not erase all these treasures. He knows that he is beautiful in his knightly garb, dressed in the wonders of the road. He knows that his sandals have allowed him to become one with the road. He knows that Fileo can whisper in his heart. He has had this intimate and personal experience.

It is dark, very dark. Bartholomew searches deeper within himself. He has the spirit of the victorious, the strength of the bold and the perseverance of the brave. He is the knight Bartholomew. He has walked a lot. He has learned much. He has marvelled. Even in the night. He searches, and little by little he finds in himself the light of Anne-Marie, her smile, her humour, and her wonderful book that never leaves her. He listens. He listens again. He perceives the snake's slither, the slither moves away behind him as he moves forward. He listens. He listens, and there he hears the small steps of Fileo's hooves. He rejoices in his night. He only has to walk to the sound of his friend's footsteps.

Bartholomew listens. He follows the sound of the little lamb's steps. Fear goes away. With closed eyes, the knight walks with a light heart. In his heart, Fileo guides him. No harm can come to him now. Bartholomew knows that the victory he has been dreaming of is close at hand. He is confident. Yes, the brave knight Bartholomew trusts in the discreet and muffled sound of the lamb Fileo's hooves.

Blessed is he who listens: even in the dark
He walks in peace.

This treasure of life is trust.

The arrival

The knight Bartholomew arrives in a beautiful meadow bathed in light. The castle is there, immense and marvellous before him. A thin fence surrounds it, the small gate is open, Fileo is there waiting for his friend. Suddenly, a ray of light zaps the sky and touches Bartholomew's heart. This light illuminates his mind and in a flash he understands: Fileo. Fileo had been there all along the way. It was as if this path, this path of life on which he, a brave knight, had walked, this path was both his own path and the path of Fileo. It was as if Fileo himself had unrolled the path to the rhythm of his steps.

Fileo is not only the path. He looks at him there, a little further down, at the castle gate. Fileo is the door. The knight would never have got there without Fileo. Bartholomew feels very small in front of this majestic castle, and that is sweet in his heart. He is a small knight, full of great desires for victory and happiness. He is happy to be small, because Fileo holds the door open for him and he is going to enter this unique and exceptional world.

Fileo looks at Bartholomew and smiles at him. He seems to be waiting for him, without disturbing this moment of eternity. The knight approaches. He walks, it is no longer he who leans on the earth, it is the earth that seems to carry him. He stops at the gate of the fence and looks at Fileo. The lamb's gaze has never left him and Fileo says to him softly, "Bartholomew, Bartholomew, come in here. Bartholomew, I love you so much." Bartholomew's heart overflows with joy, "Thank you Fileo, my friend, my brother, thank you. I love you too, every second of my life, day and night!"

In the courtyard, the table is set. Everyone, the fawn Matteus, the princess Anne-Marie, Fileo, and he, Bartholomew, are received like kings! Fileo announces that a distinguished guest is coming, he comes to join the table and meet the joyful group in person. He is the architect of this marvellous castle, the one who has prepared every last detail for each companion. They are all beaming with happiness. Smiles on their lips, joy in their hearts. Anne-Marie winks at her knight friend. Bartholomew knows that the architect is much more than an artist, a builder, a creator. He is a father who joins them and takes care of them, "My friends, let us feast!"

One morning...

The morning dawns. Bartholomew, the fawn Matteus, Anne-Marie and Fileo faded away. The light came in slowly through the edge of the curtain and Caspar opened his eyes. He is in his room, the castle banquet was a dream. A dream so real though. Caspar is still in his bed, his breathing is deep, his feet are no longer agitated under his duvet, thoughts no longer whirl. Caspar feels at peace. A new day begins. He feels as if he can feel the stones in Bartholomew's sandals. He stays under his duvet for a while longer. It is as if, in his own heart, this morning, he found a little knight and a princess full of wisdom.

Caspar savours this moment, when the sun rises and the house slowly wakes up. The alarm clock has not yet rung. He sees every pebble in his dream again, big, small or sharp. There are always pebbles on a long road and yet Caspar feels more at peace and stronger this morning. He feels as if he too has walked this path and discovered the value of gentleness, generosity and perseverance. He is still the same, in his room, but the confidence and joy he has seen in the friends of his dream give a new taste to the beginning of this day.

Today is Thursday. Small steps or big steps, the day will tell, but this prospect of a marvellous castle waiting for him and of a benevolent architect who would take care of every detail of the adventure, pleases him a lot. It makes him smile, there, warm under his duvet.

Really, his dream castle was so beautiful. Each of the friends in his dream was so beautiful. The path itself was so beautiful. Walking, working, laughing, stopping, playing, watching. Caspar hears Mum and Dad's footsteps at the end of the corridor. It reminds him of the sounds of Fileo the lamb's hooves. This dream is like a treasure for his day! This dream has given him the key, one tiny word that protects all eternity: love.

Contents

About the author

Caroline Moulinet has a Master's Degree in Chemistry. She worked for several years in the Cosmetics industry in France before moving to England. Married with four children, she created Radiance Partners Ltd to help women fulfill their vocation as mothers. A journalist for Aleteia, she is also an author. She talks to mothers about three keys to parenting in 'Pause, and change your perspective'. Her book 'A Mother's Heart, Spirituality of a Mother' shares how a woman's heart is a privileged place to better discover the heart of God and to live in his tenderness. In 'Caspar's dream', she uses the form of a dream to show the path of a life, the Evil and the sins that have entered into Creation, the virtues to be discovered and practised throughout one's existence, the goodness of Christ who encourages and cares for each person in order to draw each soul towards Love and divine Happiness.

Printed in Great Britain
by Amazon

11225776R00047